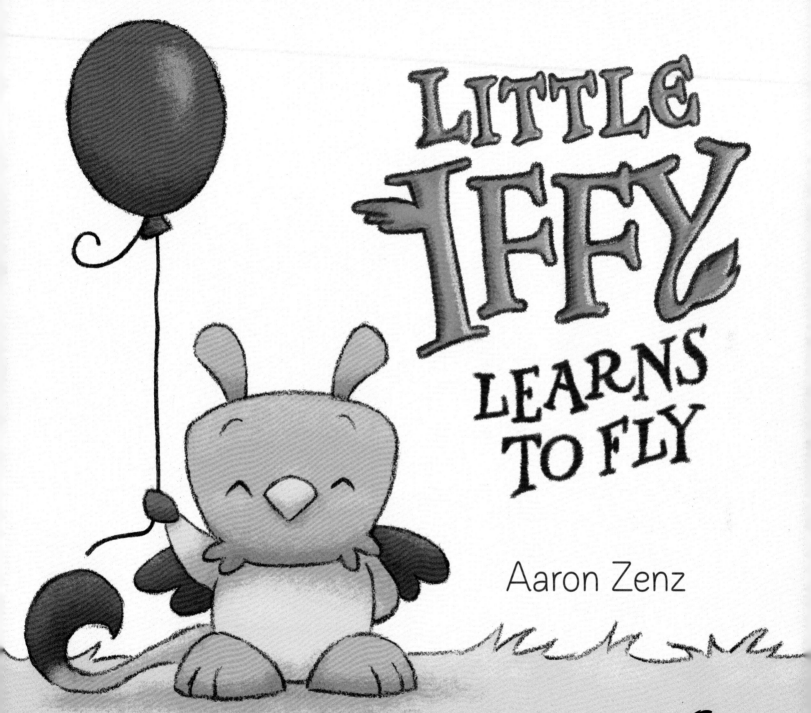

LITTLE IFFY
LEARNS TO FLY

Aaron Zenz

two lions

Little Iffy is a bitty griffin.

Griffins are part lion
and part eagle.

Iffy's friends
can't wait for him to use
those wings and learn to fly.

But Little Iffy
is a little more chicken
than eagle . . .

buzz...

... and flying means up.
Very, very up.

What if he goes up
and never comes down?

Iffy likes **down**.
Down feels safe.

Down is always best.

But not to worry!
Eggs Pegasus will get him to fly.
She has a plan.

Eggs is **always** hatching a plan.

"Here's the plan!" says Eggs.
"Swing up and
flap your wings, Little Iffy!"

"No, thank you. Down is best."

"Here's the plan!" says Eggs.
"Climb back up and flap your wings, Little Iffy!"

"No, thank you.
Down is best."

"Here's the plan!" says Eggs.

"We'll lift you up,
and you flap your wings,
Little Iffy!"

Iffy goes to the down-est place he can find.

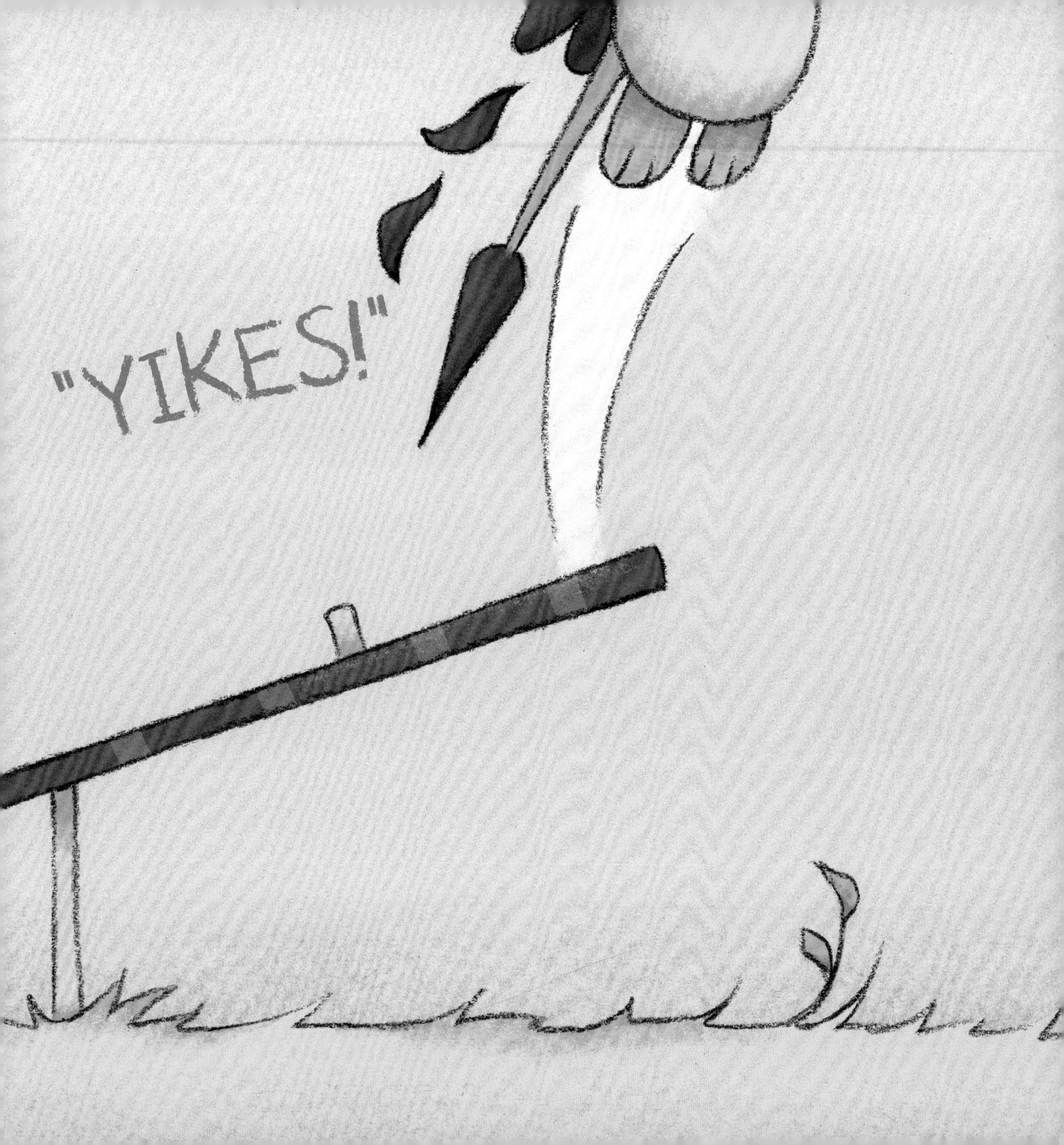
"YIKES!"

"Well, THAT wasn't part of the plan," says Eggs.

"OH NO!!!"

Iffy comes **down**.

Very, very
down.

Maybe **down** isn't always best.

Now Little Iffy knows
not to worry about up ...

... because
Eggs IS always
hatching a plan!

For my biggest fan, Gracie
—from your biggest fan, Dad

Published by Two Lions, New York

www.apub.com

Amazon, the Amazon logo, and Two Lions are trademarks of Amazon.com, Inc., or its affiliates.

ISBN-13: 9781503939868 (hardcover)
ISBN-10: 1503939863 (hardcover)

The illustrations are rendered in digital media.

Book design by AndWorld Design
Printed in China

First Edition
10 9 8 7 6 5 4 3 2 1

buzz...